MAGICAL CREATURES

GROOVY TUBE BOOK™

Fact Book · Creatures · Game Board

by Kate Torpie · Illustrated by John Shroades

Conceived, developed, and designed by innovativeKids®
Game by innovativeKids®
www.innovativekids.com
Copyright © 2007 by innovativeKids®
All rights reserved

Published by innovativeKids®,
A division of innovative USA®, Inc.
18 Ann Street
Norwalk, CT 06854
Printed in China
10 9 8 7 6 5 4 3

ISBN 10: 1-58476-619-0
ISBN 13: 978-1-58476-619-3
Not for individual sale.
Figures designed by
Joshua David McKenney

Pegasus

Fenghuang

Firebird

Phoenix

Siren

Centaur

Mermaid   Bunyip

Fairy

Unicorn

Banshe

Hippogriff

Baku

Hanuman

Gnome

Hippocampus

Encantado

2

THE MAGICAL WORLD

Throughout time and around the world, people have told stories of magical creatures and their unbelievable, otherworldly powers. For instance, Brazilian myths tell of a creature that has the power to change from a dolphin into a human being when it leaves its watery home. The ancient Greeks wrote about beautiful sea maidens whose sweet singing voices cast spells on passing sailors. Arab legend tells of a spirit that grants wishes when it's caught. The Russians spoke of a bird who sings a song that can cure almost any illness. And to this day, Japanese children keep statues by their bedside of a spirit with the power to eat nightmares.

These are just a few of the creatures that have long fascinated humankind. Read their stories inside. Learn their traits. Then it's up to you to decide what you believe is real—and what is just *fantasy*.

Elf

Pixie

Ghoul

Genie

Naga

Brownie

Leprechaun

Satyr

Nymph

THE WONDERS OF THE SKY

THE PHOENIX

The ancient Greeks told of an amazing bird called the phoenix (FEE-niks). When the phoenix feels its death is near (every 500 to 1,461 years), it builds a nest and then lights it on fire. As the flames engulf the dying phoenix, a new, young phoenix soars up from the ashes. There is only one phoenix alive in the world at any one time.

THE FENGHUANG

The immortal but rare fenghuang (FENG-wang) rules over all birds. Its appearance signals good luck and peace. The fenghuang lives high atop the Kunlun Mountains in northern China. It appears in good times but hides during times of trouble.

THE FIREBIRD

The firebird flies by shooting flames. It has glittering crystal eyes, and pearls spill from its beak when it sings. Hearing its song can heal the sick and help the blind see. The firebird also gives magical apples as gifts. Russians believe that eating an apple from a firebird will make you young and beautiful forever.

Winged Wonders

Once, a Greek warrior forced Pegasus to fly him to Mount Olympus, the home of the Greek gods. No mortal was allowed on Mount Olympus. So Zeus, the king of the Greek gods, sent an insect to bite Pegasus. When it did, Pegasus bucked the warrior off its back and flew into the sky to become a constellation.

PEGASUS

Pegasus (PEG-uh-sis) was born from the blood of Medusa after Medusa was beheaded. Pegasus was a winged horse with the power to inspire poets, painters, and musicians. Once, it stamped its hoof, and a magical spring of water burst from the ground. A single sip from this spring gives artists great ideas.

Griffins

Griffins (GRI-finz) are part eagle and part lion. Though the typical griffin is only as large as a wolf, it is strong enough to carry an elephant. Griffins also mate for life. If a griffin's partner dies, the widowed griffin will spend the rest of its life alone. Griffins' talons are prized throughout Asia because they can be used to detect poison.

Griffins make their nests from gold and precious gems. They use their long talons and powerful lion's legs to fend off anything that tries to steal their treasure!

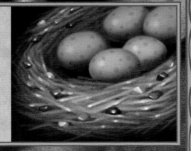

Hippogriffs can fly faster than lightning! If a knight has a hippogriff to ride, he's always able to escape danger.

Hippogriffs

Hippogriffs (HIP-uh-grifs) are the offspring of a griffin and a horse. Griffins and horses are known to hate each other, so hippogriffs are extremely rare. Hippogriffs have the talons, wings, and head of an eagle, like a griffin, but the back legs and tail of a horse. And yet, hippogriffs are not fierce. In fact, some medieval knights even kept them as pets.

7

Fairyland

Fairyland is where many small, magical creatures live. Fairies travel back and forth to Fairyland through secret doorways throughout western Europe. Humans also can travel to Fairyland if they can find a door. But if a human eats or drinks something while in Fairyland, he or she can never leave. Also, time moves much slower in Fairyland. An hour in Fairyland is the same as years in the human world.

Brownies

Every brownie has a family to watch over. They help with chores and bring magic and luck. Anyone in the house can hear the noise brownies make at night while they're cleaning, but brownies are rarely seen—and then only by children. When brownies get angry, they can get mean. Brownies often will wake up messy guests with a smack!

Pixies

More than anything, pixies enjoy practical jokes! They love stealing horses at night (and returning them by morning), sending people in the wrong direction, and throwing rocks. But even when they mean well, they tend to make a mess of things. Pixies can be identified by the shimmery pixie dust that follows behind them. They also have pointy ears and noses.

Circles of toadstools often sprout after pixies have a party.

LEPRECHAUNS

Leprechauns (LEP-pri-kahnz) hide their pots of gold at the ends of rainbows. If a human catches a leprechaun by his coattails, the leprechaun has to give up all his gold! A caught leprechaun will offer three wishes to get his gold back. Keep the gold—leprechauns are known for being tricky about wishes. Leprechauns also have a job: they make shoes for all of Fairyland!

FAIRIES

Fairies are beautiful, magical creatures. They have human features, but can be as small as 3 inches (7 cm). Female fairies are said to be able to forecast births and deaths.

GNOMES

Gnomes (nomez) look like hunch-backed old men. Gnomes can't go outside during the day. Sunlight turns them into toads or rocks. Gnomes live underground, and their homes have no front doors. That's because gnomes can walk right through dirt and rocks. Gnomes are also very smart, but they only share what they know with other gnomes.

Half Human

Centaurs

Centaurs (SEN-torz) are as smart as men and as strong as horses. These two parts of their identity are often at war with one another. Part of every centaur wants to act like a man, but another part wants to follow its animal instincts. Unfortunately, its animal side usually wins out.

One centaur named Chiron (KY-ron) was different from the others. He was thoughtful and virtuous. Chiron even gave up his immortality to give to humankind.

Chiron was killed by the Greek hero Heracles (HARE-ah-cleez). Heracles was trying to stop some evil centaurs from rioting, and Chiron accidentally got in the way of a poisoned arrow. Since Chiron was so good and died so unjustly, the gods placed him in the sky as the constellation Sagittarius.

Nagas

Nagas (NAH-gaz) are snake gods. They are cobralike and have one or more heads. Nagas have nasty tempers, but they generally treat humans well as long as humans treat Earth well. Nagas' main duty is to guard treasures and make rain. According to Hindu stories, some nagas have married humans. Their descendents are some of the most respected Indian families.

Satyrs

Satyrs (SAY-terz) are gods of forests and mountains. They are known for making mischief. In fact, one of their most popular activities is chasing nymphs. Pan is the most famous satyr in Greek and Roman mythology. Like all satyrs, he spent his days frolicking in the woods, dancing, and chasing nymphs.

Sometimes, satyrs take their fun too far. They like to scare mortals who are lost in the woods at night, and they have been known to make noises that drive some people crazy. The word "panic" even comes from Pan's name.

11

Unicorns

Unicorns have been spotted in locations across the world. They are smaller than horses and more delicate. They have a single, spiral-shaped horn and a white beard, like a goat's. Unicorns are good, but wild and fierce. Only a young girl with the purest heart can tame a unicorn.

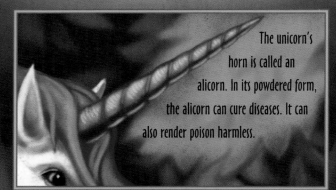

The unicorn's horn is called an alicorn. In its powdered form, the alicorn can cure diseases. It can also render poison harmless.

Syrinx was a dryad, a forest nymph, who Pan loved to chase. Hearing her pleas, the gods helped her escape Pan's grasp by transforming her into reeds. Pan then cut the reeds and fashioned them into the first panpipe.

Mysterious

Elves

Elves look like tiny humans and are best known for their power of invisibility and their mischievous nature. Elves cause disease, give people bad dreams, and have even kidnapped human children. That said, some elves are good ones who lead quiet lives, help humans, and are at peace with nature. Good elves are called "light elves," while evil elves are called "dark elves."

Nymphs

Nymphs (nimfs) are female spirits hidden throughout the natural world who help protect Earth. The ancient Greeks noted many different types of nymphs, each of whom live in a different place. For instance, *oreads* (OR-ee-adz) are mountain nymphs, *hamadryads* (ham-ah-DRY-adz) are tree nymphs, and *leimoniads* (lay-MON-ee-adz) are meadow nymphs. Nymphs live as long as the natural thing they protect does. So for instance, when a tree dies, its hamadryad dies, too.

Dark elves are known to kidnap human children. When they do, they leave behind a changeling—a deformed troll, fairy, or elf baby. It is easy to detect a changeling, though. Just cook a meal in an eggshell. The changeling will say, "I have seen the acorn before the oak, but I never saw the likes of this," and vanish, to be replaced by the missing baby.

Under the Sea

Poseidon is the ancient Greek god of the sea and of earthquakes. His weapon is called a trident, which he carries with him everywhere.

Nereids

A nereid (NIR-ee-id) is a sea nymph. There are fifty nereids. They are able to tell the future. Together with their father, the ancient Greek god Nereus, they have saved many ships from sinking in the seas around Greece.

Nereids are playful and friends to all sea animals. They love to ride dolphins and help sailors who have run into trouble.

Hippocampi

Hippocampi pull Poseidon's (puh-SY-dun) chariot. With their strong front legs, hippocampi create mountainous waves. But a second flick of their slick, scaly tails flattens waves, leaving smooth water behind. This is how Poseidon moves about the ocean quickly and invisibly.

14

Mermaids

Mermaids are known for their lovely singing voices. Just hearing their sweet voices has caused sailors to fall in love and jump overboard into the sea, never to be seen again. The sight of mermaids playing in the waves has distracted sailors and caused many shipwrecks.

On occasion, a sailor has married a mermaid. To do so, the sailor must steal the mermaid's comb or mirror. As long as the sailor keeps the object hidden from her, the mermaid must stay with him.

The Wicked Ones

Sirens

Sirens are often confused with mermaids. Like mermaids, sirens have the head of a woman and beautiful singing voices. But instead of a fish's tail, sirens have the body of a bird. Sirens are also pure evil. According to the ancient Greeks, they use their sweet voices to lure sailors to the sirens' island, where their ships crash on the rocky shore. Then, the sirens kill and eat the sailors trapped on board.

The sirens' island, said to be off the coast of Italy, is littered with sailors' bones.

The Bunyip

Among the Aborigines of Australia lives a creature called the bunyip. The bunyip is made from parts of many different animals. As a result, the bunyip never looks the same twice. The bunyip attacks anyone who comes near its home. At night, this evil beast hunts for women and children!

Aborigines are the native people of Australia. Aborigines' traditions are based on Dreamtime stories. These stories tell how Earth and the Aborigines came to be. In one Dreamtime story, the bunyip loses its eye during a fight. Aborigines believe that the full moon is the bunyip's lost eye, watching over them.

Ghouls

Ghouls (goolz) live in graveyards and other empty places throughout the Middle East. They are known to rob graves and eat the dead. Ghouls constantly change shape, but they always can be identified by their hooved feet.

Shape Shifters

Selkies

A selkie (SEL-kee) can change from a seal to a human simply by taking off its sealskin. When it is ready to become a seal again, it must get its skin back. To keep its cast-off sealskin safe, the selkie will hide it in the rocks along the British shoreline. If a person finds a selkie's skin and steals it, the selkie cannot return to the water. Instead, it must be a servant to the person who stole its skin.

In human form, selkies are always beautiful. Men and women often fall in love with them. If a selkie has children with a human, its children also will be shape-shifters.

Kelpies

A person who sees a lone, shadowy horse standing by the waters off Great Britain should take a close look into its eyes before riding it. If its eyes look blank, it isn't a horse— it's a kelpie (KEL-pee)! If a kelpie lures a person onto its back, it leaps into the sea and drowns its passenger!

Kelpies can also appear in human form when out of water. But pieces of seaweed mixed in the kelpie's hair give it away.

Encantados

Encantados (en-kan-TAH-dos) are dolphins that have the ability to become human. They love human company—especially at parties. If they hear a party going on, they will leave the water, change to human form, and join in the fun. Encantados are very popular at parties because of their supernatural musical abilities. Because encantados try to keep their identity a secret, they rarely stay long. Partygoers have reported seeing a guest dash from a party and turn into a dolphin just as he or she jumped into a river.

Encantados occasionally get lonely. They have been known to fall in love with humans. Encantados will sometimes kidnap the person it's fallen in love with just to be with him or her.

Otherworldly Wonders

Nahuals

Nahuals (nah-HWALZ) are spirits that guard and protect Native Americans during the day. Each nahual watches over one person. During the night, that nahual turns into an animal. Either it will leave its person and wander around or help its person complete unfinished tasks. If a nahual is killed, the person it protects will die, too.

When European settlers came to the Americas, they were terrified of nahuals and hunted them. They thought the nahuals would cause them to lose battles against the Native Americans.

BANSHEES

A banshee (BAN-shee) may appear either as an old woman in rags or as a woman washing blood out of her clothes in a river. More often, she is not seen at all—just heard. Her cry can sound like that of a woman in mourning or like a strong wind. Those who hear her cry should beware—according to the Irish, her song warns of death!

There are five types of genies. Some are more powerful than others. It is impossible to know which type of genie you've found unless you ask it, and even then, it might not tell you the truth.

GENIES

Genies (JEE-neez) are made of "fireless smoke." Like people, they have free will and can do what they want. But when a person traps a genie, the genie must make that person's wishes come true! According to Middle Eastern mythology, genies are usually trapped in bottles or oil lamps.

KINDLY SPIRITS

In Japan, some children keep a little baku statue next to their bed. Keeping a baku next to the bed scares off nightmares and helps bakus find children who need them.

BAKUS

Bakus (BAH-kooz) are watchful spirits. They have an elephant's head and a lion's mane, feet like a tiger's, and a tail like a cow's. Bakus eat nightmares. Sometimes, hungry bakus seek out nightmares on their own. Other times, a person needs to wake up and whisper, "Baku, eat my dreams!" Their magic transforms bad dreams into good luck.

Hanuman

Hanuman (hah-NEW-mon) has the face of a monkey, but he stands like a human. Hindus believe that he is the son of the wind god and is able to fly and create whirlwinds. He is much stronger than mortals and can change his size and shape as he wants.

When he was young, Hanuman used his power to create mischief. He would make whirlwinds and giggle as important people were blown around. When he got older, Hanuman put his powers to good use. Once, he was asked to find a life-saving herb. Hanuman flew up to the mountains, but he didn't know which herb to grab. To make sure he brought back the right one, he carried the whole mountain with him!

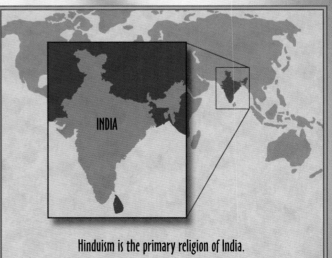

Hinduism is the primary religion of India.

Players: 2–4

Object of the Game

A shipwrecked sailor has fallen in love with a selkie. She wants to return home to the sea, but he has hidden her sealskin somewhere on the island. A magical creature is guarding it. Your goal is to determine who is guarding the skin and where it is hidden. You must make your way around the island, gathering clues until you find the skin and defeat the guardian creature.

Setting Up

Choose a creature from among the ones in the tube to be your game piece.

Photocopy the list on the right or write down the name of each creature and each area of the island on a piece of scrap paper.

Shuffle the creature cards. Take the top card and, without looking at it, place it facedown. Shuffle the island cards. Take the top card and, without looking at it, place it facedown next to the creature card. These cards show which creature is guarding the selkie skin and where the selkie skin is hidden. The rest of the island and creature cards should be distributed as evenly as possible among the players. (Some players may receive more cards than others.) Each player should hold their cards so that no other player can see them.

Save the Selkie

Island Cards (8)

- ☑ Beach
- ☑ Caves
- ☐ Cliffs
- ☑ Flower Fields
- ☐ Forest
- ☐ Lagoon
- ☑ Waterfall
- ☐ Volcano

Creature Cards (15)

- ☐ Banshee
- ☐ Centaur
- ☐ Elf
- ☐ Fairy
- ☐ Fenghuang
- ☐ Genie
- ☑ Hanuman
- ☐ Hippocampus
- ☐ Hippogriff
- ☐ Mermaid
- ☑ Naga
- ☐ Pegasus
- ☑ Phoenix
- ☐ Satyr
- ☐ Unicorn

Playing the Game

Spin the spinner. Whoever spins the highest number goes first. That person should spin the spinner again and move that number of spaces. Players can move in any direction they wish.

Entering an Area of the Island

There are two ways to enter an area of the island:

1. By spinning the spinner and moving your creature along the squares and entering through an opening. You do not have to spin the exact number of spaces to enter. (For example, if you spin a 5, you can still enter an area that is four spaces away.)
2. By using a magic passage. You can move this way without spinning the spinner.

Exiting an Area of the Island

There are two ways to exit an area of the island:

1. By spinning the spinner and moving your creature out through an opening.
2. By landing on a magic passage. You can move around the board this way without spinning the spinner.

You may not stay in an area of the island for more than one turn.

Making a Hypothesis

Each time you enter a new area of the island, you can gather clues about who is guarding the selkie's skin and where it is. You can do this by making a hypothesis, or a guess. Your hypothesis should name which creature you think is guarding the selkie's skin and what area